Knight School

adapted by Daphne Pendergrass

based on the screenplay "Mike the Knight and the Knight School"

Simon Spotlight

New York   London   Toronto   Sydney   New Delhi

SIMON SPOTLIGHT
An imprint of Simon & Schuster Children's Publishing Division
1230 Avenue of the Americas, New York, New York 10020
First Simon Spotlight paperback edition July 2015
© 2015 Hit (MTK) Limited. Mike the Knight™ and logo and Be a Knight, Do It Right!™ are trademarks of
Hit (MTK) Limited. © 2015 HIT (MTK) Limited/Nelvana Limited, a United Kingdom-Canada Co-production
SIMON SPOTLIGHT and colophon are registered trademarks of Simon & Schuster, Inc.
For information about special discounts for bulk purchases, please contact Simon & Schuster
Special Sales at 1-866-506-1949 or business@simonandschuster.com.
Manufactured in the United States of America 0615 LAK
10 9 8 7 6 5 4 3 2 1
ISBN 978-1-4814-3690-8
ISBN 978-1-4814-3694-6 (eBook)

Mike, the dragons, Evie, and their friends, Robin and Marion, were playing hide-and-seek in the Arena. "Hide quickly!" Evie whispered, giggling.

Suddenly the Great Waldorfini appeared. "Time for your wizard class back at the castle, Evie!" he called.

Evie ran from her hiding spot to join her teacher. "I *love* my wizard class—it's always so much fun!"

But just as the friends said good-bye to Evie, Mike had an idea! "Evie's off to have fun at wizard class—why don't we have fun at *knight* class?" he said.

"By the King's crown, that's it!" Mike said, jumping into the stands. "I'm Mike the Knight, and my mission is to teach Robin, Marion, Sparkie, and Squirt to be great knights!"

Mike quickly put on his armor and went down to the stable to get Galahad, but when he pulled out his sword, it was a Hula-Hoop!

"A Hula-Hoop? Evie!" Mike said, shaking his head. "Oh well. Time to start my Knight School! To the Arena!"

Sparkie and Squirt brought in school desks for everyone to sit at, and a chalkboard for Mike to write his lessons on. Marion, Robin, and Squirt settled into their seats just fine, but Sparkie was way too big for his desk! The others giggled as Sparkie balanced the desk on his tummy.

Mike wasn't happy with all the laughter. "Pay attention, everyone! Knight School lesson number one—knightly spy practice."

Mike pointed to the drawing on his chalkboard. "This is how you stand to be a knightly spy. Make sure no one *sees* you spying."

The dragons, Robin, and Marion all went off to practice their knightly spying. "Come with me," Squirt said. "We'll be the hidden spies looking for Sparkie!"

And with that, the three of them hid behind the chalkboard and peeked out for Sparkie. Squirt got into his spying pose, but Marion and Robin couldn't stop laughing!

"Robin and Marion, you're not doing the knightly spy
pose!" Mike tried to show them how to stand, but they just
giggled and giggled.

"You're making lots of noise too. Anyone could hear you
and know where you are!" But it was no use—Robin and
Marion were just too silly. Mike was frustrated, so he decided
to move on to another subject.

Mike moved the class to the other side of the Arena, where a jump was set up for Galahad. "Next lesson: Leaping over things that are in your way. Watch this!" Mike got on Galahad and galloped over the jump. The class cheered!

"Well done, Galahad!" He turned to the class, "Now you all try!"

Robin and Marion tried to run and jump over the obstacle, but it was much too high for them.

"No problem!" Marion shouted to the dragons. "Get ready to catch us!"

Robin and Marion grabbed a springboard and dragged it over to the front of the jump. The spring helped them bounce perfectly over to the other side—they even did a flip!

"Huzzah!" Marion and Robin shouted together. "Well done!" Sparkie cried.

But Mike was not happy—that wasn't how he'd taught them to jump! "It *does* look like fun, but I just don't think it's something *knights* would do," he said.

Mike started to walk away, but Squirt stopped him. "Robin and Marion just want to play, Mike. That's why they came here today."

"They *can* play, Squirt, just in a knightly way. Now it's time for jousting!" Mike called the class over to the jousting area. "I'll show you how!"

Mike charged with his lance out. It knocked the shield perfectly.

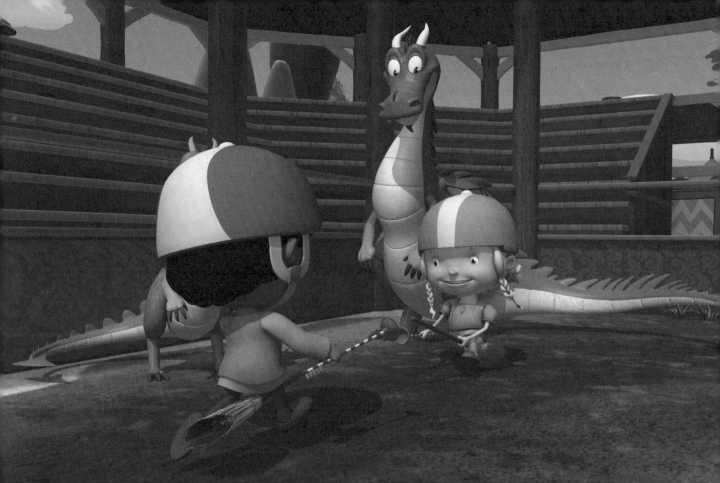

"Before you try on Galahad, you need to practice on the ground," Mike said to the class.

"We don't need Galahad!" Marion said, laughing. "We can have hobby horses!"

Marion and Robin got on a pair of broomsticks and pretended to joust each other with sucker arrows. Before long all the friends were laughing, but Mike was even more upset— no one was doing what he'd taught them!

"Come and join in, Mike!" Sparkie called.

"It does look like fun," Mike began. "But knights would never use their lances like that. Can't we just try the lesson one more time? If none of you will learn to be knightly, I won't finish my mission! Watch me joust one more time."

Mike got onto Galahad and charged again. But he forgot to duck after he hit the shield, and the weight sent him flying high up onto the arch over the Arena's entrance!

"Help! I'm stuck!" cried Mike.

"We know what to do!" Marion said.
The friends worked together to drag the springboard over to the entrance.

Robin and Marion ran and jumped onto the springboard together, soaring all the way up to the arch where Mike was stuck. Then they each grabbed Mike by the arm and floated back down into Sparkie's arms.

"What an amazingly knightly rescue!" Mike exclaimed.

"Robin and Marion were knightly *and* had fun at the same time," Squirt said.

"I shouldn't have worried about everyone playing while they were learning—you can be knightly and laugh too!" Mike said.

Mike drew his Hula-Hoop sword and gave it to Squirt who held it high in the air. The three friends took turns jumping off the springboard and through the Hula-Hoop!

"Woohoo, huzzah!" Mike shouted to his friends as they flew through the air.

Evie soon arrived back at the Arena with the Great Waldorfini. "Wow!" she said. "I had a great time in my wizard class, but your knightly class looks just as fun, Mike!"

"I've never had so much fun—maybe I'll run Knight School every day!" Mike said.

The friends cheered. Learning new things together was the most fun of all!